To my deux unbelievable enfants, Casey and Jake—J.S.

To my planet Corona amikos: Rory, Steve-o, Mark-o and the Beck—L.S.

BALONEY
(HENRY P.)

received and decoded by Jon Scieszka

visual recreation by Lane Smith

GRAFICA MOLLY LEACH

VIKING

Last Tuesday morning, at 8:37 a.m.,
Henry P. Baloney was finally late for class once too often.

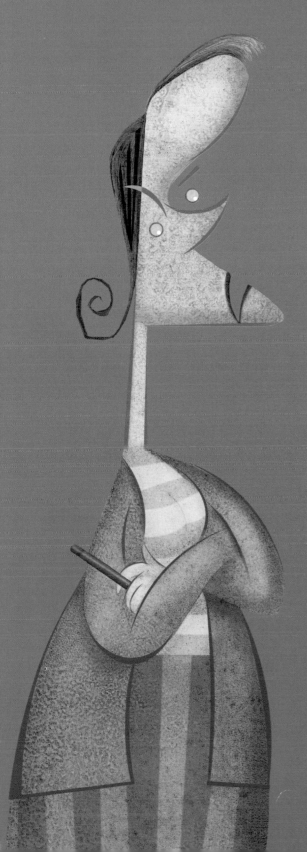

"That's it," said Miss Bugscuffle. "Permanent Lifelong Detention ... unless you have one very good and very believable excuse."

"Well I would have been exactly on time," said Henry.

"But ...

I MISPLACED MY TRUSTY *ZIMULIS.*

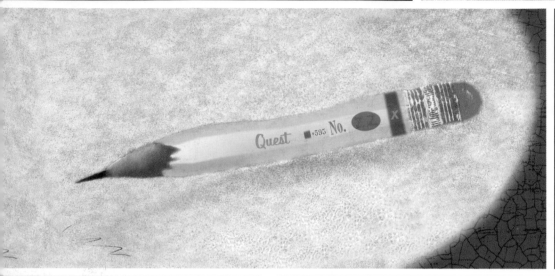

THEN I ... UM ... FOUND IT ON MY *DESKI.*

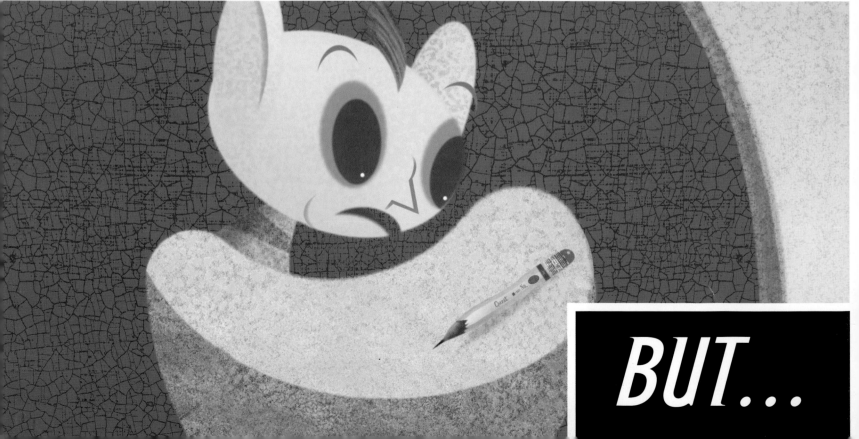

BUT...

SOMEONE HAD PUT MY DESKI IN A TORAKKU.

THE TORAKKU DROVE ME RIGHT HERE TO SZKOLA. BUT...

THEN IT DROVE RIGHT PAST.

I GRABBED MY ZIMULIS AND JUMPED OUT.

BUT...

I JUMPED

SMACK IN THE

MIDDLE OF A...

RAZZO
LAUNCH
PAD.

190

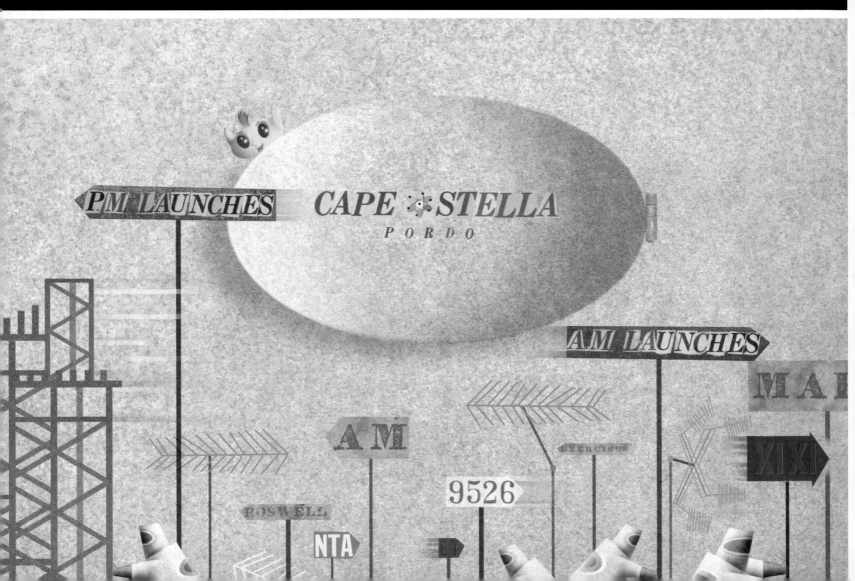

I USED MY ZIMULIS TO POP OPEN THE ESCAPE PORDO. BUT...

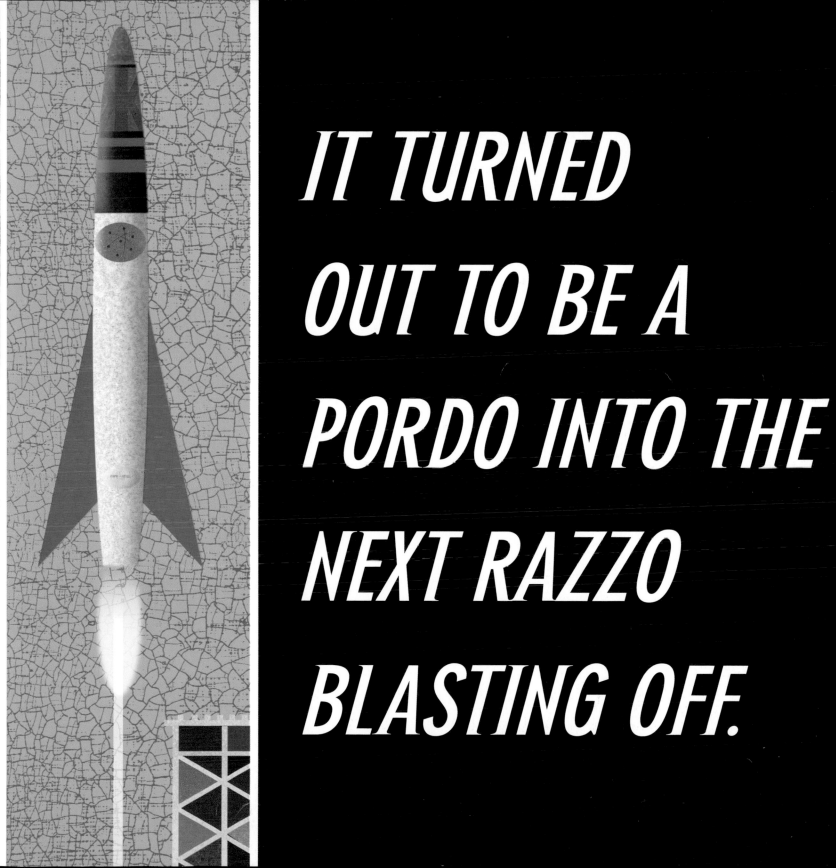

I JAMMED THE RAZZO CONTROLS WITH MY ZIMULIS SO I COULD LAND BEHIND SZKOLA AND STILL BE ON TIME. BUT...

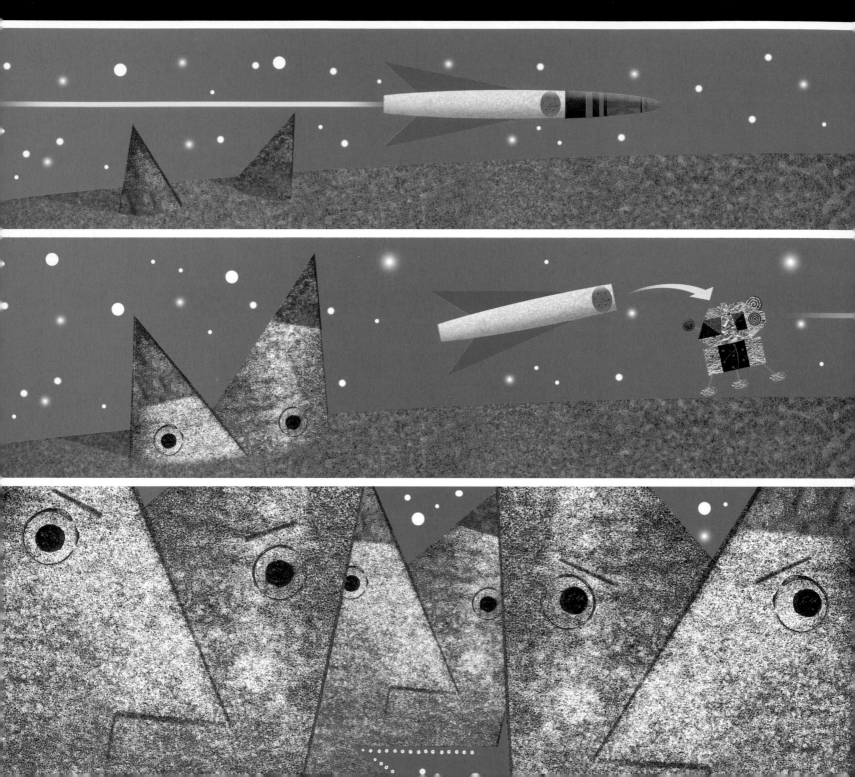

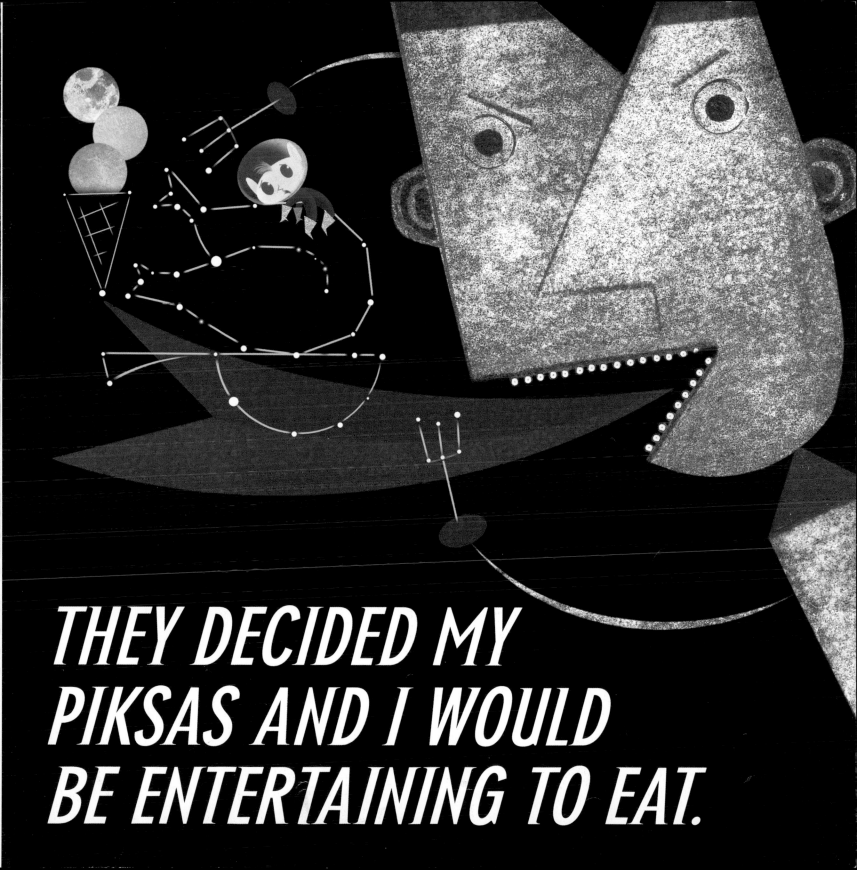

THEY DECIDED MY PIKSAS AND I WOULD BE ENTERTAINING TO EAT.

I CHANGED THEIR MINDS WITH GIADRAMS AND CUCALATIONS SO FANTASTIC THEY...

CROWNED ME KUNINGAS OF THE WHOLE PLANET.

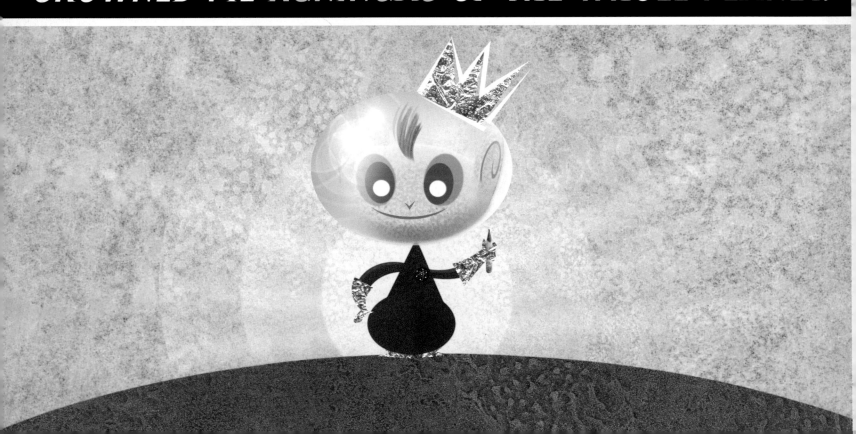

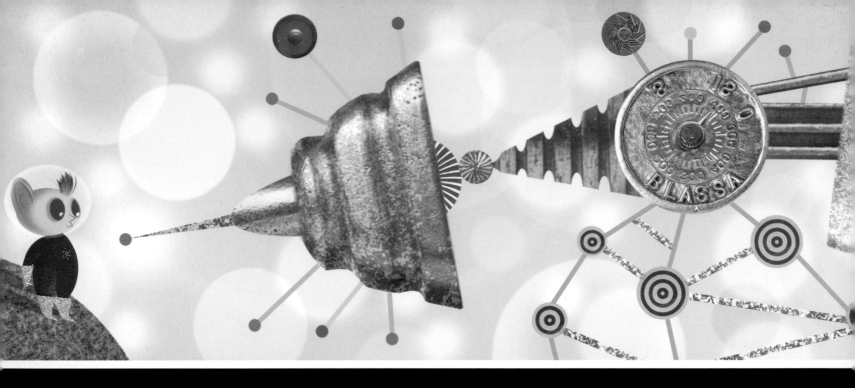

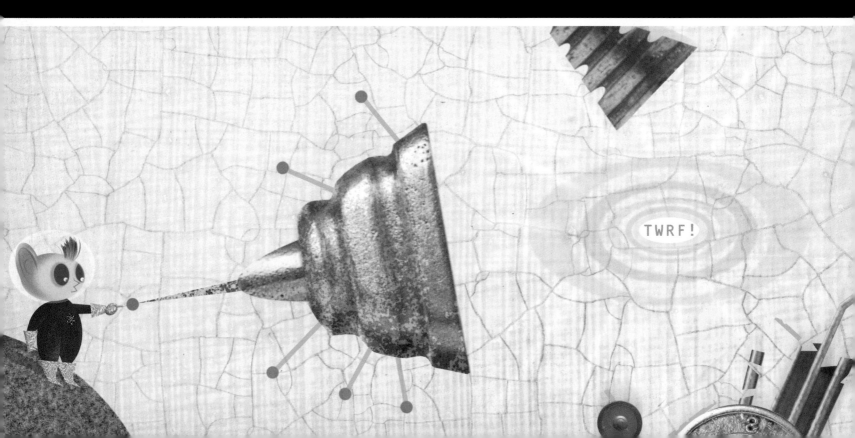

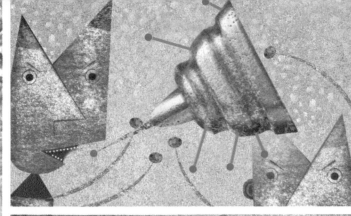

THEIR BLASSA WITH MY ZIMULIS.

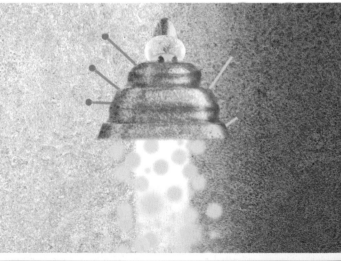

BUT...

THEY MADE A NEW PLAN TO SEND ME BACK IN A SIGHING FLOSSER ...

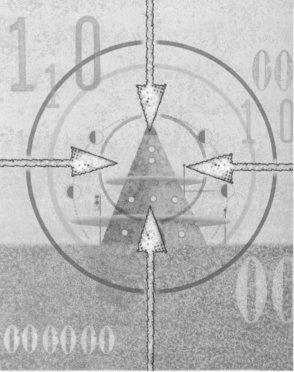

TO FRACASSE OUR SZKOLA.

I ALSO ERASED THE SIGHING FLOSSER PORDO LOCK AND FELL OUT.

I DROPPED

LIKE AN

UYARAK.

"I WAS ONLY THREE SECONDS AWAY FROM ZERPLATZEN ALL OVER THE SPEELPLAATS. NOT EVEN MY TRUSTY ZIMULIS COULD SAVE ME."

"So what did you do?" said Miss Bugscuffle. "How could you possibly save yourself?"

"I suddenly remembered ...

THAT FALLING BODIES OBEY THE LAW OF GRAVITY.

AND I HAVEN'T LEARNED THE LAW OF GRAVITY YET. SO I STOPPED AND CAME TO SZKOLA.

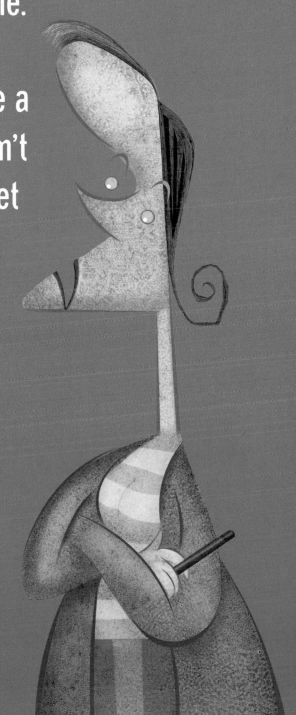

All of which made me exactly seven minutes late this aamu."

"Henry P. Baloney," said Miss Bugscuffle. "That is unbelievable. But today's assignment is to compose a tall tale. So why don't you sit down and get started writing."

"I'd love to," said Henry. "But . . .

I SEEM TO HAVE MISPLACED MY ZIMULIS."

This transmission was received directly from
deep space. Once the signals were decoded,
it became clear that this was a story about
a lifeform similar to many Earthlings. Even
more amazing was the discovery that the
story is written in a combination of many
different Earth languages including Latvian,
Swahili, Finnish, Esperanto, and Inuktitut.

Who knows why.

DECODER

AAMU *(Finnish)* morning
ASTROSUS *(Latin)* unlucky
BLASSA *(Uqbaric)* raygun
BUTTUNA *(Maltese)* button
CUCALATIONS *(Transposition)* calculations
DESKI *(Swahili)* desk
FRACASSE *(French)* shatter
GIADRAMS *(Transposition)* diagrams
KUNINGAS *(Estonian)* king
PIKSA *(Melanesian Pidgin)* picture
PORDO *(Esperanto)* door
RAZZO *(Italian)* rocket
SIGHING FLOSSER *(Spoonerism)* flying saucer
SPEELPLAATS *(Dutch)* playground
SZKOLA *(Polish)* school
TORAKKU *(Japanese)* truck
TWRF *(Welsh)* noise
UYARAK *(Inuktitut)* stone
ZERPLATZEN *(German)* splattering
ZIMULIS *(Latvian)* pencil

© 2001

VIKING
Published by the Penguin Group
Penguin Putnam Books for Young Readers, 345 Hudson Street, New York, New York 10014, U.S.A.
Penguin Books Ltd, 27 Wrights Lane, London W8 5TZ, England
Penguin Books Australia Ltd, Ringwood, Victoria, Australia
Penguin Books Canada Ltd, 10 Alcorn Avenue, Toronto, Ontario, Canada M4V 3B2
Penguin Books (N.Z.) Ltd, 182–190 Wairau Road, Auckland 10, New Zealand

Penguin Books Ltd, Registered Offices: Harmondsworth, Middlesex, England

First published in 2001 by Viking, a division of Penguin Putnam Books for Young Readers

1 3 5 7 9 10 8 6 4 2

Text copyright © Jon Scieszka, 2001
Illustrations copyright © Lane Smith, 2001
All rights reserved

LIBRARY OF CONGRESS CATALOGING-IN-PUBLICATION DATA
Scieszka, Jon.
Baloney, Henry P. / received and decoded by Jon Scieszka ; visual recreation by Lane Smith.   p. cm.
Summary: A transmission received from outer space in a combination of different Earth languages
tells of an alien schoolboy's fantastic excuse for being late to school again.
ISBN 0–670–89248–3 (hardcover)
[1. Life on other planets--Fiction. 2. Schools--Fiction.] I. Smith, Lane, ill. II. Title.
PZ7.S41267 Bal 2001 [E]--dc21 00–012041

Printed in Hong Kong
Set in Global

JJ

$15

Every illustration, tasweer, duab, eglureb, kuva, and whakaahua was
composed by human, machine, machine-assisted human, and/or human assisted machine.

DESIGN: Molly Leach, New York, New York

DATE DUE

MAY 20			
MAY 23			
JUN 10			
JUN 20			
JUL 08			
SEP 08			
OCT 08			
NOV 10			
NOV 19			
DEC 18			
JUN 08 / JAN 13			
MAR 10			
APR 15			
APR 16			
GAYLORD			PRINTED IN U.S.A.